"We can't give them Dil's formula!" said Tommy. "Dil needs it. If he doesn't have formula, what's *he* gonna eat?" Tommy stood up proudly. "He's my little brother, and I gotta look out for him, you guys. And you know what? I think those are bad growed-ups. Good growed-ups ring the doorbell instead of trying to climb through a window."

"So what are we going to do, Tommy?" asked Phil.

Rugrats Chapter Books

The Perfect Formula

The Perfect Formula

by Sarah Willson
illustrated by Mel Grant

SCHOLASTIC INC.

New York Toronto London Auckland Sydney
Mexico City New Delhi Hong Kong

Chapter 1

"Come on, Stu, we don't want to be late again," called Didi from the top of the basement stairs. Stu and Didi were Tommy Pickles's parents.

"Just a minute, Deed!" Stu answered. He was hunched over his workbench, furiously scribbling down numbers and mathematical symbols.

Didi walked down a few steps. She had Tommy's baby brother, Dil, in her arms. "Stu dear, Chas, Betty, and Howard are ready to go! The weekly Lipschitz Parenting Seminar starts in half an hour! If we keep getting there late, they'll think we're bad parents!"

"Aw, but, Deed . . . I'm so close to perfecting the formula for this edible finger paint. It's *definitely* the invention that will put Pickles Industries on the map!"

Stu was an inventor. His basement workshop was full of toys and gadgets, all in various stages of creation. He held up a container of red goo for Didi to see. "Strawberry!" he exclaimed. He dipped his finger in and tasted the goo. "Ugh," Stu muttered as he made a face. "I'm still working out the flavor proportions." He looked at his formula, erased something, and then wrote down something else.

"It's lovely, Stu," said Didi, who was busy peeking into Dil's diaper. "But you

can finish it when we get back. The grandparents are all here, ready to baby-sit the kids!"

Stu heaved a sigh and looked at his formula again. Quickly he scribbled down a few more numbers. "But, honey, I've *got* to hurry! At the toy convention I went to last week, I heard that the Tupper brothers are working on the exact same kind of finger paint technology! If I don't get this formula perfected soon, they will beat me to it! I tell ya, Deed, the toy business is a bunny-eat-bunny world. You have to stay ahead of the competition or they'll knock you right off the map!"

"Stu, you promised!"

Stu sighed again and pushed his chair back. He followed Didi slowly up the stairs.

Didi's parents, Boris and Minka, were

arguing about what jacket Dil should wear.

"It's the middle of July!" cried Boris.

"July-shmy. These babies don't dress warmly enough. You want him to freeze to death?" protested Minka as she held up a heavy baby-sized coat.

Stu's father, Lou, shook his head. "Why, when I was a baby, we didn't even *have* coats. I had to wear *fifteen* burlap grain sacks to keep warm!"

But Minka wasn't listening. "And vhat about eating? They don't eat enough! Look how thin they are, the poor dahlinks!"

She pointed to Tommy, Phil, Lil, and Chuckie, who were sitting quietly in the playpen, watching the grown-ups. "The poor things only eat when I visit. I am going to cook for them today—good food!" Minka added.

"Thanks for reminding me, Mom," said Didi. "I almost forgot to pack Dil's formula!"

She picked up a bottle and tucked it into the pocket of the diaper bag. Then she stooped down to give Tommy a kiss. "Bye, sweetheart!"

"Be good, kids!" barked Phil and Lil's mother, Betty.

"Bye, Chuckie!" called Chuckie's dad, Chas.

"Thanks for watching the kids, Dad!" Stu said to Grandpa Lou. "Oh, and don't forget to water the lawn, okay?" Then finally the grown-ups and Dil were out the door.

"You sprouts play. I'm going to watch the ball game," said Grandpa Lou, settling down on the couch and turning on the television.

"I vant to look for some scrapbooks

up in the attic," said Boris, heading for the stairs.

"Today I cook just for you, *kinderlach,* just like last week," said Minka. "I vill make you something good, something from the old country."

She looked at the babies and shook her head sadly. "So thin," she murmured as she bustled off to the kitchen.

"Tommy, your grandma's gonna feed us old food!" Chuckie said when the babies were alone. "It's gonna be worse than last time!"

"Are we going to have to eat it?" asked Phil. "'Member how Chuckie spit up the lotsas she cooked?"

"'Member the purple stuff she put in our bottles last time she baby-sitted for us?" said Lil.

"Yeah, I 'member," Tommy said grimly. "She called it 'borusht.'"

The babies shuddered.

"We gotta think of a plan," said Tommy. "That food is not good for us."

He took out his plastic screwdriver and unlatched the playpen. "I'll go look out the window. Maybe I'll find some squirrels or somethin' that we can feed it to."

The other babies watched him go.

"Should we help him look for squirrels?" asked Lil.

"Okay. But first let's go play with shaving cream, Lil," said Phil.

"I want to play restaurant, Phil!" Lil said.

"Shaving cream, Lillian!"

"Restaurant, Philip!"

"Shaving cream!"

"Restaurant!"

The twins wandered off, still arguing.

"I'm scared of squirrels, Tommy," said

Chuckie. He took out his marbles and began to toss them on the floor. "Wanna play marbles instead?" he asked his friend.

"You go ahead, Chuckie," replied Tommy. "I'll be right back."

Tommy toddled toward the window. He looked out. Something was staring right at him.

It was someone's face!

Chapter 2

"Waaaaaah!" wailed Tommy. He stared back at the face in the window. The face had weaselly eyes, a pointy chin, and a surprised expression.

Tommy wailed again. But Grandpa Lou had turned down his hearing aid and was asleep on the couch. Boris was upstairs in the attic. And Minka was whirring the blender in the kitchen.

Through the screened window

Tommy heard the face speak.

"Hank! I thought you said no one would be here!" it whispered loudly. "There's a bunch of babies in there! And an old guy asleep on the couch, and I think I hear someone else in the kitchen!"

The face in the window disappeared. Another face took its place. This face was pink and pudgy. It looked at Tommy. Then IT spoke.

"That's what I heard Pickles say at the convention last week, Frank! He said he wasn't going to be around today. He had to go to some seminar. How'd I know he'd leave a house full of people behind?"

The two men stood in the bushes under the window. Frank, the one with the weaselly face, was tall and skinny. He wore a silly plaid suit. Hank was

short and plump, and he wore red suspenders, which held up baggy purple pants. He also had a big bouquet of flowers in his pudgy fingers.

"By the way, Frank, why do I need to carry these flowers?" asked Hank.

"If someone sees us, they'll think we're just delivery guys, get it?" replied Frank. "I got the camera hidden in the wrapping paper."

"So what should we do now?" asked Hank.

"I say we break in anyway," Frank replied. "Pickles is way ahead of us with the bubble technology. We HAVE to have that formula! It will put Tupper Toys on the map! Besides, we're not going to let some babies and a sleepy old guy stop us, are we, Hank?"

"Well, okay, Frank," said Hank. "Why don't we go around back and try to get in through the kitchen door?"

Hank and Frank disappeared from the window.

The twins were helping Chuckie set up marbles by the front door. Tommy hurried over to them.

"Hey, you guys!" Tommy panted. "Guess what I just saw!"

"Squirrels?" asked Phil.

"Nuh-uh. There are two strange growed-ups outside. They're trying to get into the house!"

"Why don't they just ring the doorbell, Tommy?" asked Chuckie.

"They're hiding. I think they don't want anyone to see them," replied Tommy. "They said they wanted some formula . . . hey, maybe they're hungry!"

"Then why don't we give them some of Dil's formula?" said Chuckie.

"We can't give them Dil's formula!"

said Tommy. "Dil needs it. If he doesn't have formula, what's *he* gonna eat?" Tommy stood up proudly. "He's my little brother, and I gotta look out for him, you guys. And you know what? I think those are bad growed-ups. Good growed-ups ring the doorbell instead of trying to climb through a window."

"So what are we going to do, Tommy?" asked Phil.

"I don't know, but we gotta think of something to feed those two growed-ups so they don't take my brother's formula," said Tommy.

Suddenly Minka burst into the room, dusting flour from her apron. "Almost lunchtime, my little dahlinks!" she announced. "So thin," she muttered again before heading back into the kitchen.

"Tommy, this is TERRIBLE!" moaned

Chuckie. "We got hungry bad guys who are trying to get inside the house. And your grandma is going to feed us borusht and weird stuff all day long!"

Tommy looked at Chuckie and Phil and Lil. Then he smiled. "That's it, Chuckie!"

"What's it, Tommy?"

"We'll give them my grandma's food. Then *we* won't have to eat it—and maybe the hungry bad guys will go away!"

Chapter 3

Grandpa Lou awoke and half-opened his eyes. "You squirts playing nice?" he asked the babies. Then he jumped up. "Leapin' lizards! Almost forgot I promised your dad I'd water the lawn."

He turned and pointed the TV remote control toward the window. Outside, the lawn sprinklers suddenly began spurting water.

"That son of mine sure has a way

with gadgets," said Grandpa Lou admiringly. "Hey, how'd you kids get out?" He got up from the couch, put the babies back into the playpen, and latched it. Then he walked back to the couch and lay down. Soon he began to snore.

The babies heard coughs and splutters coming from outside.

"I'm drenched, Frank!"

"Yeah, me too, Hank."

"It's not good for my sinuses, Frank."

"Never mind that, Hank. I hear the grandma leaving the kitchen. Let's go."

"Time to eat, *kinderlach*," Minka called. She unlatched the playpen. Then she herded the babies toward the kitchen.

As Tommy toddled into the kitchen, he caught a glimpse of Hank peeking in through the sliding-glass doors.

Tommy's dog, Spike, was lying on the kitchen floor asleep. Tommy prodded

Spike, who opened one eye and followed Tommy's gaze. When he spotted Hank, Spike let out a long, low growl. Hank ducked quickly out of sight.

Minka put Tommy into his high chair and the other babies into their booster seats. Then she set a bowl down in front of each baby. "Eat now. This is goulash. Not too hot. Delicious!"

The babies looked down at the goop in their bowls. Chuckie watched a gloppy bubble rise to the surface and slowly pop. Phil poked at something green. Lil stuck her spoon into the mush and watched the spoon slowly keel over. The babies looked at one another in horror.

"MINKA!" It was Boris calling from the attic.

"Vhat now!" bellowed Minka. Then she sighed and turned to the babies. "You eat, my *kinderlach*. I'll be right

back." Minka bustled out.

"Quick, you guys," said Tommy, slipping the screwdriver out of his diaper and unlatching his high chair. He slid down and walked over to Spike's dog dish. "Sorry, boy," he said. Tommy tipped his bowl of goulash into Spike's dish. It took a long time before the thick glop finally landed in the dish with a sickening SPLAT!

Spike let out a whimper and then a whine. The rest of the babies passed their bowls down to Tommy. He dumped their goulash into the dog dish too.

"Wuh-wuh-wuh-WOOOOOO!" howled Spike.

Tommy patted Spike's head. Then he walked over to the kitchen door. He slid it open and shoved the dish of goulash onto the back stoop. "Maybe those hungry growed-ups will like this," he said.

Outside, Hank and Frank waited near the kitchen doors. The sprinkler had soaked them from head to foot. Hank sneezed again.

"Come on, Hank," whispered Frank. "The grandmother has left the kitchen. It's just the kids in there now. Let's try getting in this way."

Squelch, squelch, squelch went their soggy feet as they tiptoed toward the sliding-glass doors. Hank still clutched the bouquet of flowers in one hand.

Just as they stepped up to the patio, they heard a strange sound.

"Wuh-wuh-WOOOOOO!"

Hank looked at Frank in terror. "They've got a vicious attack dog, Frank!" he cried. He turned to run. His foot landed in the dish of goulash. Spike's dish flipped over and flew into the air. Goulash splattered all over Hank and

Frank. The rest of it oozed over the patio.

Falling backward, Hank landed on his backside. Frank began waving his arms wildly like a windmill, trying to keep his balance in the slippery mush. But it was no use. He fell with a thud. Both men slipped and slid right off the patio. Then they clambered into some bushes to hide.

"Did they like the stuff your grandma made, Tommy?" called Phil from his booster seat.

Tommy was peeking outside, trying to catch a glimpse of the two men. "Uh-huh," he replied. "They went away. Spike's dish is empty. They must like the goo-lots. Dil's formula is safe, you guys!" he said.

Out in the bushes Hank wiped a glop of goulash from his forehead. He licked his finger. "Not bad," he said.

Frank squeezed some water from his plaid suit. Then he turned to his brother. "Let's try the window in the living room again," he muttered. "We've got to get that formula."

Chapter 4

Minka bustled back into the kitchen. She looked at the empty bowls in front of the babies. "Wonderful!" she clapped. "You like Grandma Minka's goulash, yes? Last week you didn't even touch it. Now I vill make some nice dumplinks for you! Run along and play."

She helped them out of their booster seats, then shooed the babies out of the kitchen.

Chuckie was worried. "What are dumb lings?" he asked.

"I dunno, Chuckie," Tommy said. "But they sound worse than goo-lots."

"Do you think the bad guys are really, really gone, Tommy?" asked Lil.

Tommy nodded, just before they heard a tiny scratching sound. The babies looked up. Frank had unlatched the screen and was climbing in through the window! The babies looked over at Grandpa Lou.

He was snoring gently.

Suddenly Frank let out a howl. "AAAAAAAH!" he yelled. "I'm BLEEDING!"

Sure enough, Frank's clothing was covered with red splotches. He slid back out of the window.

"Gee, Frank," they heard Hank say. "Can I have your corner office if you don't pull through?"

They heard Frank howl again, and then their voices faded into the distance.

"Uh-oh," said Phil.

"Uh-oh," said Lil.

"What's the matter?" asked Tommy.

"I guess we got a little ketchup on the windowsill when we were playing restaurant," admitted Lil.

"It was *your* idea to play restaurant, Lillian."

"Was not, Philip."

"Was too!"

"It looks like they're still hungry, Tommy," Chuckie pointed out. "They're still trying to get Dil's formula. I don't like this one bit."

Minka came out carrying a big plate. "Dumplinks for you, my little pumpkins!" she trilled. She set the plate down next to the babies and went back into the kitchen.

Chuckie looked at the plate. "I can smell 'em, even with my stuffy nose," he said.

"Listen!" said Tommy. "I hear the bad guys. They're back!"

The babies listened. Sure enough, they could hear noises coming from the bathroom window.

"We gotta stop them," said Tommy.

"But, Tommy," said Chuckie, "it's too dangerous."

Tommy looked at Chuckie. "Dil needs our help, Chuckie. Who laughs even when nothin's funny? Dil. And who spits up the bestest? Dil."

"I guess you got a point, Tommy."

"So let's grab some of these dumb lings and get to that bathroom and feed those bad guys!"

The babies grabbed fistfuls of dumplings. They hurried into the bathroom.

"Help me up, you guys," said Tommy. Phil and Lil hoisted him up to the window. They handed him the squished-up, greasy dumplings, which he laid out carefully on the windowsill.

Then the babies hurried out of the bathroom, leaving the door half open. They sat down by the doorway to listen.

Soon Hank and Frank were jimmying open the bathroom window and climbing inside. Hank picked up a dumpling. "Mmm! You should try one of these, Frank!" he said to his brother.

"Never mind those, Hank," said Frank. "Now that we're in the house, we have to find a way down to the basement. I remember Pickles said he had a basement workshop. The formula must be down there."

"And this Jell-O is good too," said Hank.

"Hank, that's not Jell-O. It's hair gel."

Suddenly they heard someone coming. Frank stepped into the bathtub and immediately slipped and fell flat on his face. Hank stepped in right after him and fell on top of his brother. He pulled the shower curtain closed.

Grandpa Lou walked in. "Now, where did I put those teeth of mine?" he muttered to himself. "Ah, here they are."

Grandpa Lou put his teeth into his mouth and walked out.

"Frank!" whispered Hank. "You're foaming at the mouth! In fact, you're foaming all over the place!"

Frank just moaned.

Outside the bathroom door Phil and Lil looked at each other. "*You're* the one who wanted to play with shaving cream in the bathtub, Philip," said Lil.

"Was not!"

"Was too!"

Minka came over to where the babies were sitting.

"Achoo!" said Hank from inside the bathroom.

Minka looked down at the babies. "Tch! Vich one of you just sneezed? I vill steam up the bathroom! Good for your little stuffy noses!"

Minka walked into the bathroom and reached into the shower. She turned on the water full force and walked back out, latching the door behind her.

Hank and Frank climbed soggily out of the tub. Water dripped from every part of them. "Now we're locked in, Frank," snuffled Hank.

"Come on, Hank," said Frank. "Let's get out of here. We'll try the bedroom window."

Chapter 5

Minka was delighted that the babies had eaten all of her dumplings. "You dahlinks go upstairs and play in Tommy's room!" she said happily. "Next I vill make my special latkes!"

"Oh, no, not the lotsas," Chuckie whimpered softly as Minka helped them up the stairs.

"Boris!" Minka bellowed toward the attic. "Come down and vatch the little ones vile I go cook them some delicious latkes!"

Alone in Tommy's room the babies were trying to decide what to do next.

"I think those guys are still hungry, Tommy!" said Phil. "Did you hear them say they're still gonna try to get in here?"

"Why don't we just give them some formula?" said Lil. "Then maybe they'll go away."

"No," Tommy replied. "We *gotta* save that for my baby brother. The growed-ups can eat other kinds of food. We just gotta keep feeding them. We gotta . . . aaaaah!"

He'd glimpsed a face at the window. It was upside down this time. Outside on the roof Hank was holding on to Frank's feet. It was Frank who peered into the window. "Hold on tight!" Frank said to

his brother. "I'm just going to open this window. . . ."

Just then Grandpa Boris walked into Tommy's room carrying a photo album.

"Did I ever show you childrinks this album from the old country?" he asked. "Come, sit. I show you."

The babies gathered around.

Frank's face began to turn pinkish, then grew purple.

"Aaaah. This is vere I grew up as a little boy . . ." Boris began.

Up on the roof Hank was beginning to perspire. His hands shook as he tightly clutched his brother's ankles. "Can't . . . hold . . . on . . . much . . . longer!" he muttered through clenched teeth.

"And this! This is the shop vere your great-uncle Shlomo and your great-grandpapa used to vork," Boris continued.

Crash!

Chapter 6

"BORIS!" yelled Minka from downstairs. "Did you hear something outside?"

Boris looked at the babies and shrugged. "Must be that crazy neighbor cat again. Come, ve go look."

Outside, Hank and Frank had landed in a large bush. "You okay, Frank?" asked Hank.

"I guess so, Hank," replied Frank. "You still have the camera?"

Hank started feeling around in the bushes.

Plonk!

The bouquet of flowers rolled off the roof and fell on his head. He picked them up and rubbed his head. "Yep, it's still here, hidden in these flowers."

"Good," said Frank. "Look, the grand-mother has left the kitchen doors wide open! She's standing in the backyard. Let's get down to that basement!"

Hank and Frank scrambled out of the bushes. They crept along the back of the house and then scooted into the kitchen. Glancing warily over at Grandpa Lou asleep on the couch, they crawled across the living room toward the basement.

Boris was just coming downstairs with the babies. Tommy spied Hank and Frank ducking down into the basement, but Boris wasn't paying any attention.

Minka came into the living room. "That cat must have run avay," she told Boris. "Come. Help me grate some potatoes." They went into the kitchen.

Tommy looked at his friends. "The hungry bad guys are in the basement!" he said.

"But there's no formula down there," said Lil.

"No, just my dad's stuff," Tommy replied. "They must think that's where the formula is."

Hank and Frank tiptoed down the basement steps. "This must be Pickles's workshop," said Hank, looking around. "And THIS must be the edible finger paint!" he said excitedly.

He picked up a bright green container,

unscrewed the cap, and tasted the goo in it. "Mmm!" he said. "Lime flavoring! Or is it dill pickle?"

"Now we have to find that formula," whispered Frank, looking around. "We'd better hurry—Pickles might be home soon."

The two brothers rummaged around. Then Frank saw Stu's notepad with all the numbers and symbols on it. "BINGO!" he cried triumphantly.

"Frank, this is no time for playing bingo," scolded his brother.

"Nooooo!" replied Frank. "I mean I found it! Get that camera over here!"

Hank pulled out a tiny camera from the bouquet of flowers he was still clutching. He handed it to Frank, who snapped picture after picture of Stu's formula.

Then he took more pictures of the

finger paints. Frank handed the camera back to Hank, who hid it in the flower stems.

"Take good care of that camera," Frank warned his brother.

Quietly they crept back up the stairs. When they reached the top, they opened the door softly and looked around. "Just the kids," whispered Frank. "The old guy is still asleep on the couch."

The babies watched Hank and Frank crawl toward the front door. Softly the brothers opened it. They stood up slowly, then—*Crash!*

Frank was sprawled across the doorway. Hank spun around in a circle, whirling his arms and legs. Then his feet shot up into the air, and down he came. *Kablam!*

The bouquet of flowers flew into the air and landed on top of Hank. Hank

landed on top of Frank, who began to moan.

"Uh-oh," said Chuckie, staring at the heap. "I guess we left my marbles all over the floor, huh, Tommy?"

The noise finally awakened Grandpa Lou. "What in tarnation?" he said, leaping from the couch.

Minka and Boris came running in from the kitchen. They all stared at Hank and Frank, who lay across the doorstep looking dazed.

Chapter 7

"How nice!" said Minka. "Somebody sent flowers!"

She stooped down and picked up the bouquet that was lying on top of Hank. She tore off the wrapping paper and plunked the flowers into a vase that was sitting on a nearby table.

"I vill go fill it up with water," she said and walked into the kitchen. They all heard water running.

"The c-c-camera!" stammered Frank. "It'll be soaked!"

Hank buried his face in his hands.

"Hmmm . . . no note. Those flowers must be from a secret admirer," Grandpa Lou decided. "Probably someone I met at the lodge."

"Boris!" Minka hissed loudly to her husband when she came back with the flowers in the vase. "You have money to tip these nice young deliverymen? They look like they could use the money. Look at those clothes! So dirty! And all wet, too!"

Boris reached into his pockets and turned them inside out. He shrugged and shook his head.

"I have an idea!" Minka said. "You wait here," she said to Hank and Frank, who were staggering to their feet.

"Is she going to call the police?" Hank

whispered to his brother. Frank shrugged miserably.

Minka hurried into the kitchen and came right back out again, carrying a big paper plate stacked high with brown things.

"Here you go, boys," she said. "Nice latkes, fresh from the pot. Stick to your ribs. Delicious! And you look like you could use a good hot meal, no?"

She thrust the plate into Hank's hands. Then she pushed them out the door.

The babies went to the window and looked out. Hank and Frank staggered into a truck. Then, with a squeal of tires, they sped away.

Minka looked down at the babies. "You little ones had such good appetites today!" she beamed. "And here come your parents! I vill tell them what good eaters you were!"

Sure enough, the Pickleses' van was just pulling into the driveway. The three grandparents stepped out onto the front stoop to greet everyone.

"We did it!" Tommy said to the other babies. "We fed those bad guys, and they went away! And Dil still has his formula!"

"And we didn't have to eat any of your grandma's stuff," Chuckie added.

"They must have liked her lotsas," said Tommy.

The parents walked in. "Hello, honey!" said Didi, stooping down to give Tommy a kiss. "Did you have a nice, quiet day?"

Minka smiled broadly. "The babies ate so well today!" she said. "Goulash, dumplings, latkes—" Suddenly she stopped. "Oh, my, I forgot the borscht! I vill go fill their bottles with it!"

The babies looked at one another in horror.

"Did you say borscht?" asked Chas. "I LOVE borscht!"

"Me too," said Betty as she scooped up the twins. "Come on," she called to the others. "I say we pen these pups and go have some of Minka's borscht! The kids can have mac and cheese instead."

The babies heaved a sigh of relief as everyone headed into the kitchen.

Stu went straight to the basement. "I'll be downstairs working," he called over his shoulder.

Didi carried Dil toward the kitchen. "I'll make you up a bottle of formula, honey," she crooned to Dil.

Tommy grinned at his friends.

Chapter 8

A few days later Stu and Didi were sitting at the breakfast table. Stu was reading the newspaper. Dil was in Didi's arms, slurping down a bottle of baby formula.

"How about that!" Stu exclaimed. "The Tupper brothers have quit the toy business! And I always thought Tupper Toys was my main competition, that maybe they were trying to steal my ideas."

"That's nice," said Didi absently as she wiped Dil's chin. "How did your edible finger paint invention turn out, anyway?"

"Oh, that," said Stu. "It had a few little problems. The stuff tasted great, but it kept leaving stains on my hands, the walls, the furniture—"

Stu stopped when he caught Didi's dismayed look.

"But that's okay, though," Stu went on. "I've got plenty of other ideas in the works."

He glanced at the paper again and grinned. "Hah! It says here that the Tupper brothers plan to open a restaurant soon. Your mother better watch out, Deed. Next thing you know, they'll probably be trying to steal her secret recipes!"

In the living room the babies were playing.

"Do you think those two guys will ever come back, Tommy?" asked Chuckie.

"Nah," Tommy replied. "I think they weenied themselves off formula. Now they like old food."

"But what will we do next time your grandma comes and wants to feed us?" Chuckie asked. "We won't have any bad guys to give it to."

Tommy thought about it for a minute. "I heard my mom say Dil will be ready for real food soon. We can try to feed *him* Grandma's old food!"

About the Author

Sarah Willson has written more than eighty children's books, many of them about the Rugrats! She once worked as a newspaper cartoonist, and has also been a semiprofessional basketball player. When she was a kid, Sarah dreamed of becoming an inventor—just like Stu. She also likes to cook, so writing this book about inventors and cooking was a lot of fun. She lives in Connecticut with her husband, three small children, and two large cats. In between writing funny stories, Sarah enjoys inventing ways to get her children to eat their vegetables.